Listen, My Children

POEMS FOR FIFTH GRADERS

A CORE KNOWLEDGE® BOOK

LISTEN, MY CHILDREN: POEMS FOR FOURTH GRADERS

One in a series, *Poems for Kindergartners—Fifth Graders*, collecting the poems in the *Core Knowledge Sequence*·

A CORE KNOWLEDGE® BOOK

Series editor: Susan Tyler Hitchcock
Researcher: Jeanne Nicholson Siler
Editorial assistant: Kristen D. Moses
Consultant: Stephen B. Cushman
General editor: E. D. Hirsch Jr.

Library of Congress Card Catalog Number: 00-111615
ISBN 1-890517-33-X

Printed in Canada
Design by Diane Nelson Graphic Design
Cover art copyright © by Lance Hidy, lance@lancehidy.com

CORE KNOWLEDGE FOUNDATION
801 East High Street
Charlottesville, Virginia 22902
www.coreknowledge.org

About this Book

"LISTEN, MY CHILDREN, and you shall hear . . ." So begins a famous poem about Paul Revere, written by Henry Wadsworth Longfellow in 1855. This opening line reminds us that every time we read a poem, we hear that poem as well. The sounds and rhythms of the words are part of the poem's meaning. Poems are best understood when read out loud, or when a reader hears the sounds of the words in his or her head while reading silently.

This six-volume series collects all the poems in the Core Knowledge Sequence for kindergarten through fifth grade. Each volume includes occasional notes about the poems and biographical sketches about the poems' authors, but the focus is really the poems themselves. Some have been chosen because they reflect times past; others because of their literary fame; still others were selected because they express states of mind shared by many children.

This selection of poetry, part of the *Core Knowledge Sequence*, is based on the work of E. D. Hirsch Jr., author of *Cultural Literacy* and *The Schools We Need*. The Sequence outlines a core curriculum for preschool through grade eight in English and language arts, history and geography, math, science, art, and music. It is designed to ensure that children are exposed to the essential knowledge that establishes cultural literacy as they also acquire a broad, firm foundation for higher-level schooling. Its first version was developed in 1990 at a convention of teachers and subject matter experts. Revised in 1995 to reflect the classroom experience of Core Knowledge teachers, the Sequence is now used in hundreds of schools across America. Its content also guides the Core Knowledge Series, *What Your Kindergartner—Sixth Grader Needs to Know*.

Contents

6

A Wise Old Owl

by Edward Hersey Richards

A wise old owl sat on an oak,
The more he saw the less he spoke;
The less he spoke the more he heard;
Why aren't we like that wise old bird?

The Eagle: A Fragment

by Alfred, Lord Tennyson

He clasps the crag with crooked hands;
Close to the sun in lonely lands,
Ringed with the azure world, he stands.

The wrinkled sea beneath him crawls:
He watches from his mountain walls,
And like a thunderbolt he falls.

Alfred, Lord Tennyson
1809–1892

Queen Victoria named Alfred Tennyson England's
poet laureate in 1850, and he held that post for the
next 42 years. Tennyson wrote poems about history,
such as "The Charge of the Light Brigade," about the
Crimean War, and *Idylls of the King*, about King Arthur.
In 1883, in honor of his work, the poet was made a
baron. From then on his name was Alfred, Lord
Tennyson.

from Opposites
by Richard Wilbur

What is the opposite of riot?
It's lots of people keeping quiet.

> The opposite of doughnut? Wait
> A minute while I meditate.
> This isn't easy. Ah, I've found it!
> A cookie with a hole around it.

What is the opposite of two?
A lonely me, a lonely you.

> The opposite of a cloud could be
> A white reflection in the sea,
> Or a huge blueness in the air,
> Caused by a cloud's not being there.

The opposite of opposite?
That's much too difficult. I quit.

The Arrow and the Song

by Henry Wadsworth Longfellow

I shot an arrow into the air,
It fell to earth, I knew not where;
For, so swiftly it flew, the sight
Could not follow it in its flight.

I breathed a song into the air,
It fell to earth, I knew not where;
For who has sight so keen and strong
That it can follow the flight of song?

Long, long afterward, in an oak
I found the arrow, still unbroke;
And the song, from beginning to end,
I found again in the heart of a friend.

Henry Wadsworth Longfellow
1807–1882

Henry Wadsworth Longfellow wrote poems that made people feel good. His poetry was very popular in his lifetime, not only among his fellow Americans but also overseas. He enjoyed taking a small bit of history and turning it into rhyming story, as he did in *The Song of Hiawatha* and "Paul Revere's Ride." After he died, Longfellow became the first American remembered by a statue in the Poet's Corner of London's Westminster Abbey.

I Hear America Singing

by Walt Whitman

I hear America singing, the varied carols I hear,
Those of mechanics, each one singing his as it should be, blithe
    and strong.
The carpenter singing his as he measures his plank or beam,
The mason singing his as he makes ready for work,
    or leaves off work,
The boatman singing what belongs to him in his boat,
    the deckhand singing on the steamboat deck,
The shoemaker singing as he sits on his bench,
    the hatter singing as he stands,
The woodcutter's song, the ploughboy's on his way
    in the morning, or at noon intermission, or at sundown,
The delicious singing of the mother, or of the young wife
    at work, or of the girl singing or washing,
Each singing what belongs to him or her and to none else,
The day what belongs to the day — at night
    the party of young fellows, robust, friendly,
Singing with open mouths their strong melodious songs.

Walt Whitman
1819–1892

One of nine children, Walt Whitman attended public
school in Brooklyn, New York, until he was about 11
and had to earn money for his family. He
experimented with a new kind of poetry — poetry
that did not rhyme and that had different rhythms
line to line. He picked the 4th of July as the day he
published his first book of poems, called *Leaves of
Grass*. Every few years after that, Whitman published a
new edition of *Leaves of Grass*. Each time he added
more poems and sold more copies. By the last edition,
in 1892, the book contained more than 300 poems.

I, Too

by Langston Hughes

I, too, sing America.

I am the darker brother.
They send me to eat in the kitchen
When company comes,
But I laugh,
And eat well,
And grow strong.

Tomorrow,
I'll be at the table
When company comes.
Nobody'll dare
Say to me,
"Eat in the kitchen,"
Then.

Besides,
They'll see how beautiful I am
And be ashamed —

I, too, am America.

Langston Hughes
1902–1967

By the time of his death, Langston Hughes was widely respected for having brought the voice of African Americans into American literature. He was a leader in the "Harlem Renaissance" of the 1920s, when the creativity of African-American actors, dancers, musicians, and writers in New York City caught the attention of the entire art world. In this poem, Hughes responds to Walt Whitman's poem, "I Hear America Singing."

Incident

by Countee Cullen

Once riding in old Baltimore,
    Heart filled, head filled with glee,
I saw a Baltimorean
    Staring straight at me.

Now I was eight and very small,
    And he was no whit bigger,
And so I smiled, but he stuck out
    His tongue, and called me, "Nigger."

I saw the whole of Baltimore
    From May until November;
Of all the things that happened there —
    That's all that I remember.

Narcissa
by Gwendolyn Brooks

Some of the girls are playing jacks.
Some are playing ball.
But small Narcissa is not playing
Anything at all.

Small Narcissa sits upon
A brick in her back yard
And looks at tiger-lilies,
And shakes her pigtails hard.

First she is an ancient queen
In pomp and purple veil.
Soon she is a singing wind.
And, next, a nightingale.

How fine to be Narcissa,
A-changing like all that!
While sitting still, as still, as still
As anyone ever sat!

Gwendolyn Brooks
1917–2000

Gwendolyn Brooks wrote many poems about African-American life. She was the first black person to receive a Pulitzer Prize in Poetry, which she won in 1950 for *Annie Allen,* a book of poems about a girl growing up in Chicago, just as Brooks did. When the judges gave her the prize, they congratulated Gwendolyn Brooks for writing "strong poetry" that comes "out of the heart."

The Snowstorm

by Ralph Waldo Emerson

Announced by all the trumpets of the sky,
Arrives the snow, and, driving o'er the fields,
Seems nowhere to alight: the whited air
Hides hills and woods, the river, and the heaven,
And veils the farm-house at the garden's end.
The sled and traveler stopped, the courier's feet
Delayed, all friends shut out, the housemates sit
Around the radiant fireplace, enclosed
In a tumultuous privacy of storm.

Come, see the north wind's masonry.
Out of an unseen quarry evermore
Furnished with tile, the fierce artificer
Curves his white bastions with projected roof
Round every windward stake, or tree, or door.
Speeding, the myriad-handed, his wild work
So fanciful, so savage, naught cares he

MYRIAD
Many.

NAUGHT
[nawt]
Nothing.

For number or proportion. Mockingly,
On coop or kennel he hangs Parian wreaths;
A swan-like form invests the hidden thorn;
Fills up the farmer's lane from wall to wall,
Maugre the farmer's sighs; and at the gate
A tapering turret overtops the work.
And when his hours are numbered, and the world
Is all his own, retiring, as he were not,
Leaves, when the sun appears, astonished Art
To mimic in slow structures, stone by stone,
Built in an age, the mad wind's night-work,
The frolic architecture of the snow.

PARIAN
From the Greek island of Paros. Marble quarried on Paros is known to be glistening white.

MAUGRE
[MAW-gur]
In spite of.

TURRET
A little tower.

Ralph Waldo Emerson
1803–1882

While Ralph Waldo Emerson considered himself a poet, his speeches and essays also influenced people, especially other writers. Emerson was a leader among the American "transcendentalists." Transcendentalists questioned traditional Christian beliefs and believed instead that they would find truth in the human soul and in nature. Emerson started *The Dial,* a transcendentalist magazine. In it he published the writing of Henry David Thoreau, who wrote *Walden.*

I like to see it lap the Miles

by Emily Dickinson

I like to see it lap the Miles —
And lick the Valleys up —
And stop to feed itself at Tanks
And then — prodigious step

**PRODIGIOUS
[pro-DIJ-us]
Amazing
or huge.**

Around a Pile of Mountains —
And supercilious peer
In Shanties — by the sides of Roads —
And then a Quarry pare

**SUPERCILIOUS
[soo-per-SILL-
ee-us]
Proud and
haughty.**

To fit its sides
And crawl between
Complaining all the while
In horrid — hooting stanza —
Then chase itself down Hill —

And neigh like Boanerges —
Then — prompter than a Star,
Stop — docile and omnipotent
At its own stable door —

**BOANERGES
[bo-ah-NER-jeez]
A name given to
ministers who acted like
St. James and St. John,
who wanted to destroy
those who didn't
believe in Jesus with
fire from heaven.**

**Emily Dickinson
1830–1886**

Although she is recognized today as one of the
greatest American poets, Emily Dickinson published
only eleven poems during her lifetime. She lived a
secluded life in her hometown of Amherst,
Massachusetts, going out and meeting people less
and less as she aged. She kept her poems a secret
and stored them in her dresser drawer. After her
death, her sister found more than a thousand poems
hidden away.

A Bird came down the walk

by Emily Dickinson

A Bird came down the walk —
He did not know I saw —
He bit an Angleworm in halves
And ate the fellow, raw,

And then he drank a Dew
From a Convenient Grass —
And then hopped sidewise to the Wall
To let a Beetle pass,

He glanced with rapid eyes
That hurried all around —
They looked like frightened Beads, I thought —
He stirred his Velvet Head

Like One in danger, Cautious,
I offered him a Crumb,
And he unrolled his feathers
And rowed him softer home —

Than Oars divide the Ocean,
Too silver for a seam —
Or Butterflies, off Banks of Noon
Leap, plashless as they swim.

ANGLEWORM
An earthworm,
which could be
used by an "angler"
or fisherman
as bait.

PLASHLESS
Without
splashing.

Robert Frost
1874–1963

Robert Frost was born in California but moved at the
age of ten to New England, the region with which he
was associated ever after. His poems reflect country
life and landscapes, but they also consider universal
themes like growing up and growing old, work and
friendship. In 1961 John F. Kennedy invited Robert
Frost to read during his presidential inauguration.
On that cold January day, the glare of the sun kept
the elderly poet from reading the poem he had
written for the occasion. Instead he recited another
from memory.

The Road Not Taken

by Robert Frost

Two roads diverged in a yellow wood,
And sorry I could not travel both
And be one traveller, long I stood
And looked down one as far as I could
To where it bent in the undergrowth;

Then took the other, just as fair,
And having perhaps the better claim,
Because it was grassy and wanted wear;
Though as for that, the passing there
Had worn them really about the same,

And both that morning equally lay
In leaves no step had trodden black.
Oh, I kept the first for another day!
Yet knowing how way leads on to way,
I doubted if I should ever come back.

I shall be telling this with a sigh
Somewhere ages and ages hence:
Two roads diverged in a wood, and I —
I took the one less travelled by,
And that has made all the difference.

William Blake
1757–1827

At an early age, William Blake left school and became a printer and engraver. Many of his poems were composed as visual works of art, with colorful borders and illustrations. Some were short and simple, like "The Tyger" and "A Poison Tree," which both come from his book called *Songs of Innocence and Experience*. Others were long and complicated, telling stories about mythological characters that Blake made up. Even as a child William Blake said he could see angels and talk with prophets from the Bible. Those who met him as an adult often declared him eccentric or crazy.

The Tyger
by William Blake

Tyger! Tyger! burning bright
In the forests of the night,
What immortal hand or eye
Could frame thy fearful symmetry?

In what distant deeps or skies
Burnt the fire of thine eyes?
On what wings dare he aspire?
What the hand dare seize the fire?

And what shoulder, and what art,
Could twist the sinews of thy heart?
And when thy heart began to beat,
What dread hand? and what dread feet?

SINEWS
Tendons, or taut, strong cords of connective tissue.

What the hammer? what the chain?
In what furnace was thy brain?
What the anvil? what dread grasp
Dare its deadly terrors clasp?

When the stars threw down their spears,
And watered heaven with their tears,
Did he smile his work to see?
Did he who made the lamb make thee?

Tyger! Tyger! burning bright
In the forests of the night,
What immortal hand or eye,
Dare frame thy fearful symmetry?

Blake often wrote pairs of poems, a "song of innocence" and a "song of experience" about related subjects. This poem was a "song of experience." It was mirrored by the "song of innocence" called "The Lamb," which asked similar questions, like "Little Lamb, who made thee?"

A Poison Tree

by William Blake

I was angry with my friend:
I told my wrath, my wrath did end.
I was angry with my foe:
I told it not, my wrath did grow.

And I watered it in fears,
Night and morning with my tears;
And I sunned it with smiles,
And with soft deceitful wiles.

And it grew both day and night,
Till it bore an apple bright.
And my foe beheld it shine,
And he knew that it was mine,

And into my garden stole,
When the night had veiled the pole;
In the morning glad I see
My foe outstretched beneath the tree.

WRATH
Anger.

WILES
Sneaky ways of doing things.

VEILED THE POLE
Shadowed one side of the earth.

Barbara Frietchie

by John Greenleaf Whittier

Up from the meadows rich with corn,
Clear in the cool September morn,

The clustered spires of Frederick stand
Green-walled by the hills of Maryland.

Round about them orchards sweep,
Apple and peach tree fruited deep,

Fair as the garden of the Lord
To the eyes of the famished rebel horde,

On that pleasant morn of the early fall
When Lee marched over the mountain-wall;

Over the mountains winding down
Horse and foot, into Frederick town.

Forty flags with their silver stars,
Forty flags with their crimson bars,

Flapped in the morning wind; the sun
Of noon looked down and saw not one.

Up rose old Barbara Frietchie then,
Bowed with her fourscore years and ten;

Bravest of all in Frederick town,
She took up the flag the men hauled down;

In her attic window the staff she set,
To show that one heart was loyal yet.

FREDERICK A city in Maryland, west of Baltimore.

THE GARDEN OF THE LORD The Garden of Eden, where Adam and Eve first lived.

HORDE Crowd.

How old is someone who is "fourscore years and ten," since a "score" is 20 years?

Up the street came the rebel tread,
Stonewall Jackson riding ahead.

Under his slouched hat left and right
He glanced; the old flag met his sight.

"Halt!" — the dust-brown ranks stood fast.
"Fire!" — out blazed the rifle-blast.

It shivered the window, pane and sash;
It rent the banner with seam and gash.

Quick, as it fell, from the broken staff
Dame Barbara snatched the silken scarf.

She leaned far out on the window-sill,
And shook it forth with a royal will.

"Shoot, if you must, this old gray head,
But spare your country's flag," she said.

A shade of sadness, a blush of shame,
Over the face of the leader came;

The nobler nature within him stirred
To life at that woman's deed and word;

"Who touches a hair of yon gray head
Dies like a dog! March on!" he said.

All day long through Frederick street
Sounded the tread of marching feet:

All day long that free flag tossed
Over the heads of the rebel host.

Ever its torn folds rose and fell
On the loyal winds that loved it well;

The poem "Barbara Frietchie" refers to Stonewall Jackson, one of the toughest generals who fought under Robert E. Lee in the Confederate Army during the Civil War. Whittier probably made up the story it tells about Jackson, however. Whittier wrote this poem while the Civil War was raging, but it was published after Stonewall Jackson died.

And through the hill-gaps sunset light
Shone over it with a warm good-night.

Barbara Frietchie's work is o'er,
And the Rebel rides on his raids no more.

Honor to her! and let a tear
Fall, for her sake, on Stonewall's bier.

BIER
[beer]
Grave raised above ground.

Over Barbara Frietchie's grave,
Flag of Freedom and Union, wave!

Peace and order and beauty draw
Round thy symbol of light and law;

And ever the stars above look down
On thy stars below in Frederick town!

John Greenleaf Whittier
1807–1892

Born into a poor New England family, John Greenleaf Whittier became known for patriotic poetry. He served in the state legislature and considered running for Congress, but instead decided to use his writing to fight slavery. He wrote the words for almost one hundred hymns. By the end of his life, Whittier was such a well-known poet that people in many towns celebrated his birthday as if it were a public holiday.

Battle Hymn of the Republic

by Julia Ward Howe

Mine eyes have seen the glory of the coming of the Lord:
He is trampling out the vintage where the grapes of wrath are stored;
He hath loosed the fateful lightning of his terrible swift sword:
     His truth is marching on.

Chorus.   Glory, glory, hallelujah,
           Glory, glory, hallelujah,
           Glory, glory, hallelujah,
             His truth is marching on.

I have seen Him in the watch-fires of a hundred circling camps:
They have builded Him an altar in the evening dews and damps;
I can read His righteous sentence by the dim and flaring lamps.
     His day is marching on.

He has sounded forth the trumpet that shall never call retreat;
He is sifting out the hearts of men before his judgment-seat:
Oh! be swift, my soul, to answer Him! be jubilant, my feet!
     Our God is marching on.

In the beauty of the lilies Christ was born across the sea,
With a glory in his bosom that transfigures you and me:
As He died to make men holy, let us die to make men free,
     While God is marching on.

O Captain! My Captain!

by Walt Whitman

RACK
A mass of high, wind-driven clouds or a storm.

O Captain! my Captain! our fearful trip is done,
The ship has weather'd every rack, the prize we sought is won,
The port is near, the bells I hear, the people all exulting,
While follow eyes the steady keel, the vessel grim and daring;
　　　But O heart! heart! heart!
　　　　　O the bleeding drops of red,
　　　　　　　Where on the deck my Captain lies,
　　　　　　　　Fallen cold and dead.

KEEL
The bottom of a ship, often weighted for balance.

O Captain! my Captain! rise up and hear the bells;
Rise up — for you the flag is flung — for you the bugle trills,
For you bouquets and ribbon'd wreaths — for you the shores a-crowding,
For you they call, the swaying mass, their eager faces turning;
　　　Here, Captain! dear father!
　　　　　This arm beneath your head!
　　　　　　　It is some dream that on the deck,
　　　　　　　　You've fallen cold and dead.

My Captain does not answer, his lips are pale and still,
My father does not feel my arm, he has no pulse nor will,
The ship is anchor'd safe and sound, its voyage closed and done,
From fearful trip the victor ship comes in with object won;
　　　Exult, O shores! and ring, O bells!
　　　　　But I with mournful tread,
　　　　　　　Walk the deck my Captain lies,
　　　　　　　　Fallen cold and dead.

Julia Ward Howe wrote this poem after viewing Union troops marching to battle during the Civil War. Considering it a hymn, she used many references to stories from the Bible. Walt Whitman wrote this elegy (or poem mourning a person's death) about Abraham Lincoln in 1865, the year Lincoln was assassinated.

Casey at the Bat

by Ernest Lawrence Thayer

The outlook wasn't brilliant for the Mudville nine that day;
The score stood four to two with but one inning more to play.
And then when Cooney died at first and Barrows did the same,
A sickly silence fell upon the patrons of the game.

A straggling few got up to go in deep despair. The rest
Clung to the hope which springs eternal in the human breast;
They thought if only Casey could but get a whack at that —
We'd put up even money now with Casey at the bat.

But Flynn preceded Casey, as did also Jimmy Blake,
And the former was a lulu and the latter was a cake;
So upon that stricken multitude grim melancholy sat,
For there seemed but little chance of Casey's getting to the bat.

But Flynn let drive a single, to the wonderment of all,
And Blake, the much despised, tore the cover off the ball;
And when the dust had lifted, and the men saw what had occurred,
There was Jimmy safe at second and Flynn a-hugging third.

Then from five thousand throats and more there rose a lusty yell;
It rumbled through the valley, it rattled in the dell;
It knocked upon the mountain and recoiled upon the flat,
For Casey, mighty Casey, was advancing to the bat.

There was ease in Casey's manner as he stepped into his place;
There was pride in Casey's bearing and a smile on Casey's face.
And when, responding to the cheers, he lightly doffed his hat,
No stranger in the crowd could doubt 'twas Casey at the bat.

Ten thousand eyes were on him as he rubbed his hands with dirt;
Five thousand tongues applauded when he wiped them on his shirt.
Then while the writhing pitcher ground the ball into his hip,
Defiance gleamed in Casey's eye, a sneer curled Casey's lip.

And now the leather-covered sphere came hurtling through the air,
And Casey stood a-watching it in haughty grandeur there.
Close by the sturdy batsman the ball unheeded sped —
"That ain't my style," said Casey. "Strike one," the umpire said.

From the benches, black with people, there went up a muffled roar,
Like the beating of the storm waves on a stern and distant shore.
"Kill him! Kill the umpire!" shouted someone on the stand;
And it's likely they'd have killed him had not Casey raised his hand.

With a smile of Christian charity great Casey's visage shone;
He stilled the rising tumult; he bade the game go on;
He signaled to the pitcher, and once more the spheroid flew;
But Casey still ignored it, and the umpire said, "Strike two."

"Fraud!" cried the maddened thousands, and echo answered, "Fraud!"
But one scornful look from Casey and the audience was awed.
They saw his face grow stern and cold, they saw his muscles strain,
And they knew that Casey wouldn't let that ball go by again.

The sneer is gone from Casey's lip, his teeth are clenched in hate;
He pounds with cruel violence his bat upon the plate.
And now the pitcher holds the ball, and now he lets it go,
And now the air is shattered by the force of Casey's blow.

Oh, somewhere in this favored land the sun is shining bright;
The band is playing somewhere, and somewhere hearts are light,
And somewhere men are laughing, and somewhere children shout;
But there is no joy in Mudville — mighty Casey has struck out.

This poem appears in *Through the Looking Glass*. Soon after Alice climbed through the mirror and into a backwards land, she discovered this poem in a book, although the title and first stanza looked like this:

Jabberwocky

'Twas brillig, and the slithy toves
Did gyre and gimble in the wabe:
All mimsy were the borogoves
And the mome raths outgrabe.

When Alice held the book up to a mirror, she could read the poem, but she still didn't understand it. "Somehow it seems to fill my head with ideas," she said, "only I don't exactly know what they are!" See how many words Lewis Carroll made up to put into this poem. When you read them, don't you feel a bit like Alice?

Lewis Carroll
1832–1898

Lewis Carroll was the pen name of Charles Lutwidge Dodgson, who taught mathematics at Oxford University in England. He befriended a little girl named Alice Liddell and began telling her stories about a made-up Alice who found her way into imaginary lands. Alice Liddell encouraged Dodgson to write his stories down. He did, and then he published them as two books: *Alice's Adventures in Wonderland* and *Through the Looking Glass*.

Jabberwocky

by Lewis Carroll

'Twas brillig, and the slithy toves
    Did gyre and gimble in the wabe:
All mimsy were the borogoves
    And the mome raths outgrabe.

"Beware the Jabberwock, my son!
    The jaws that bite, the claws that catch!
Beware the Jubjub bird, and shun
    The frumious Bandersnatch!"

He took his vorpal sword in hand:
    Long time the manxome foe he sought —
So rested he by the Tumtum tree,
    And stood awhile in thought.

And as in uffish thought he stood,
    The Jabberwock, with eyes of flame,
Came whiffling through the tulgey wood,
    And burbled as it came!

One, two! One, two! And through and through
    The vorpal blade went snicker-snack!
He left it dead, and with its head
    He went galumphing back.

"And hast thou slain the Jabberwock?
    Come to my arms, my beamish boy!
O frabjous day! Callooh! Callay!"
    He chortled in his joy.

'Twas brillig, and the slithy toves
    Did gyre and gimble in the wabe:
All mimsy were the borogoves,
    And the mome raths outgrabe.

Acknowledgments

Every care has been taken to trace and acknowledge copyright of the poems and images in this volume. If accidental infringement has occurred, the editor offers apologies and welcomes communications that allow proper acknowledgment in subsequent editions.

Selections from *Opposites,* poems and drawings by Richard Wilbur. Copyright © 1973 by Richard Wilbur. Reprinted by permission of Harcourt, Inc.

"I, Too" from *Collected Poems* by Langston Hughes. Copyright © 1994 by the Estate of Langston Hughes. Reprinted by permission of Alfred A. Knopf, a Division of Random House, Inc. and by Harold Ober Associates Incorporated.

"Incident" from *Color* by Countee Cullen. Copyright © 1925 by Harper & Brothers; copyright renewed 1953 by Ida M. Cullen. Reprinted by permission of GRM Associates, Inc., agents for the estate of Ida M. Cullen.

"Narcissa" from *Bronzeville Boys and Girls* by Gwendolyn Brooks. Copyright © 1956 by Gwendolyn Brooks Blakely. Used by permission of HarperCollins Publishers.

"I like to see it lap the Miles" from *The Poems of Emily Dickinson*, Thomas H. Johnson, ed., Cambridge, Mass: The Belknap Press of Harvard University Press, Copyright © 1951, 1955, 1979 by the President and Fellows of Harvard College. Reprinted by permission of the publishers and the Trustees of Amherst College.

"A Bird came down the walk" from *The Poems of Emily Dickinson*, Thomas H. Johnson, ed., Cambridge, Mass: The Belknap Press of Harvard University Press, Copyright © 1951, 1955, 1979 by the President and Fellows of Harvard College. Reprinted by permission of the publishers and the Trustees of Amherst College.

"The Road Not Taken" from *The Poetry of Robert Frost*, by Robert Frost, edited by Edward Connery Lathem, © 1969 by Henry Holt & Co., LLC. Reprinted by permission of Henry Holt & Co., LLC.

Images:
Alfred, Lord Tennyson: © Bettmann/CORBIS
Henry Wadsworth Longfellow: © CORBIS
Walt Whitman: © CORBIS
Ralph Waldo Emerson: By permission of the Clifton Waller Barrett Library of American Literature, Special Collections Department, University of Virginia Library
Langston Hughes: © CORBIS
Gwendolyn Brooks: © Bettmann/CORBIS
Emily Dickinson: By permission of Amherst College Archives and Special Collections
Robert Frost: © Hulton-Deutsch Collection/CORBIS
William Blake: © Bettmann/CORBIS
John Greenleaf Whittier: By permission of the Clifton Waller Barrett Library of American Literature, Special Collections Department, University of Virginia Library
Lewis Carroll: © Bettmann/CORBIS